# My Sister Katie

## Christine Wright

### Illustrations by Biz Hull

AUGSBURG · MINNEAPOLIS

My sister, Katie, woke me up one morning last week.

"Meg," she called, "wake up! It's seven o'clock!"

"It can't be," I told her. "You counted the beeps on the clock wrong. It's still dark."

"Is it?" she said. She sounded disappointed. "I'll go back to bed."

But when I pulled back my curtains,
I found that it wasn't dark.

And Katie was right. It was seven
o'clock. Time to get up. I ran into
Katie's room. She was in bed, trying to
sleep.

"It's daytime really," I said.

Katie opened her eyes again. "I thought so. I heard the train a little while ago. And the birds were singing. It must be a gloomy day outside. I hope the sun comes out later."

Katie only sees in bright light because she's blind. Even in good light, she only sees the shapes of things.

Although Katie can't see her clothes very clearly, she gets dressed herself. She won't let anyone help her, but she doesn't often get things on wrong.

She knows that she can feel for the labels on her sweater and jumper. The label goes in the back. But sometimes she puts on socks that don't match. She says it doesn't matter.

"Do you know, Meg," she asked as we went downstairs, "it's a special day today? Sam's coming all day and so is Bowler, his dog. Isn't it exciting?"

She was so busy talking that she forgot where she was on the stairs. "Am I near the bottom?" she asked.

"Two more to go," I told her.

"Sam's coming today," Katie reminded Mom
as soon as we came into the kitchen. "And
Bowler," she added.

Mom laughed. "I know," she said, and gave
us both a hug.

Katie especially likes hugging Mom because
she can't see her. She enjoys stroking Mom's
hair and face.

"Please may I have toast for breakfast," asked Katie, "like Dad did?"

She always knows what Dad had for breakfast, just by the smell. She knows how to use the toaster, too, but sometimes she can't find the butter. I found it for her behind the teapot.

After breakfast, we usually talk to
God.

"Let's thank God for Sam and
Bowler coming," Katie said. "Isn't it
exciting?"

"Yes," said Mom, "it will be fun,
but we must ask God to help us all
be kind and patient with them."

Not long afterwards, the doorbell rang. We ran to the door with Mom. As soon as the door was open, Bowler bounded in. He licked Katie's face and my hands and ran down the hallway.

Sam ran after him, shouting, "Come back here, Bowler!"

Katie giggled and ran after him.

"Oh, dear," said Sam's mom. "I hope they won't be too much trouble."

Mom smiled. "Don't worry. I'm sure everything will be all right."

Just then, we heard a crash from the kitchen. We ran to see what had happened. Katie and Sam were having a pretend fight with Bowler on the floor. They'd knocked a plate off the table.

"I'm sorry," said Katie. "I forgot there were things on the table."

Mom said they shouldn't be so rough with Bowler where things might get broken. When she had cleared away the broken plate, she put a blanket on the floor in case Bowler wanted to sleep. But he didn't.

After a while, Mom said we should go
outside.

"I know," shouted Sam, "Bowler can be a
guide dog for Katie. I've seen how they do it
on television. Hold on to his leash, Katie."

Mom said, "I think I'd better be a guide
person for Bowler, though, or we'll all get
lost!"

Bowler wasn't a good guide dog. He didn't tell Katie there was a street light ahead. She bumped into it and began to cry.

"Let's walk along in the usual way," said Mom. "Meg, you hold Sam's hand, and I'll hold Katie's hand and tell her where to go."

In the park, Katie ran across the grass.
"She'll bump into the trees!" cried Sam.

"Don't worry," I told him. "She knows
when to stop. She can see their shape against
the sky."

"Perhaps she hears the leaves rustling, too,"
Mom suggested.

"She won't be able to in the winter," Sam
said.

While Katie was busy by the trees, Mom
took Sam and me over to the playground.
Sam went down the slide.

"It's too bad Katie can't slide down, too,"
he said.

"Yes, she can," Mom told him. And she
called Katie. Mom kept calling until Katie had
run across the grass to us. Mom has to do
this so that Katie knows where we are.

Sam watched in amazement as Katie climbed the slide until she felt the wider step at the top. She held tightly onto the sides as she sat down, then let go and whizzed to the bottom!

There's nothing Katie can't do at the playground. She even knows not to get too near the swings.

"You can hear the swings," she always says. "When someone's swinging, you can hear the 'swish'!"

Katie, Sam, and I enjoyed ourselves at the playground, but Bowler got bored and started to bark.

"Bowler wants to go home," Mom said.

Mom was glad when Bowler went to sleep after lunch. I read some books, Mom watched the news on television, and Sam and Katie played with the dolls.

It was quiet for a while.

Then Katie yelled, "That's my favorite doll. You can't have her!"

Sam shouted, "But I don't like this one. She's ugly!"

Bowler woke up, came in, and started to bark.

Mom was upset. "What's the matter?" she asked. "What's all the noise about?"

Katie yelled, "Sam's taken my best doll, the one with the soft hair and the shampoo smell. He's hidden her and won't give her back."

Sam threw it on the floor. "Here she is, stupid!" he grumbled. He took hold of Bowler's collar and took him back to the kitchen.

"Remember how we asked God to help us?" Mom said quietly to Katie. "It was wrong of Sam to take your doll, but let's try and be patient with him and kind to him now."

When Sam came back, Mom said, "Why don't we all make some cookies? That would be fun!"

She was right. It *was* fun. Even Bowler helped by licking up the scraps that fell on the floor—but not until we'd finished. By then Katie and Sam were friends again. They went off to play together while I helped Mom clean up the kitchen.

There was more picking up to do after Sam and Bowler had gone home. Mom and I collected the building blocks while Katie put her dolls back in their box.

"Where's Susie, my favorite doll, Meg?" Katie asked me. "I can't find her anywhere."

I laughed. "Bowler took her into the kitchen. I saw her on the blanket where he slept."

"That dog!" cried Katie, and she went to find the doll.

When Dad came home, we rushed to hug him.

"Have a good day?" he asked.

"Well. . . ." began Mom.

But Katie said, "Yes! Sam and Bowler came. We had dog fights and we went to the park. And guess what? I found some acorns!"

She had, too. She took a handful out of her coat pocket to show us.

"How did you find them?" I asked. "I never found any."

"My foot found them," she explained. "They were near the trees under some crackly leaves. Aren't they beautiful? The acorns are smooth, just like fingernails. And this top feels like a toy cup."

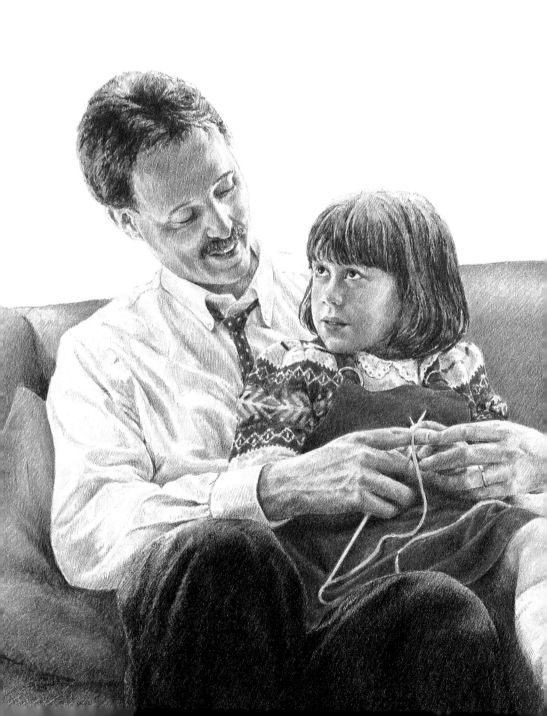

Dad is teaching Katie how to knit, but that night she was too tired to do it right. Instead, she kept talking about Sam and Bowler's visit.

"I like Sam," she said. "He knows how to play with me."

"What do you mean?" asked Dad, putting the knitting away.

"He shows me things," she explained. "And let's me see them with my hands."

When it was my bedtime, I crept upstairs in case Katie was asleep.

But she wasn't. She was singing, very sleepily, to herself.

"The world is full of lovely things.
Thank you, God.
Smells and sounds and friends and fun.
Thank you, God."

## A Note to Parents and Friends of Children

You can use this book to help your child understand more about the abilities and the problems of a blind person. You could also explore together the use of other senses apart from sight.

You might ask: How did Katie know it was morning? Why does she sometimes wear socks that don't match? You could discuss together why Katie could use the toaster, but could not find the butter. How did she know when she had reached the trees when she was in the park?

Discuss how Katie explored God's world. Talk about her friendship with Sam. How did he help her?

You can pray for people who cannot see and ask God to make your family good friends to those who are blind or who have difficulty in seeing.

It would be a good opportunity to thank God for the gift of sight and for the other senses (touch, hearing, taste, and smell) that help us to enjoy life.

### For parents with a blind or partially sighted child

You can use this book to help your child talk about how much he or she can do on his or her own. Use the example of Katie to encourage independence and thankfulness for the richness of life, even without sight.

MY SISTER KATIE
How She Sees God's World

First North American edition published 1990 by Augsburg, Minneapolis
Copyright © 1990 Scripture Union, London, England

ISBN 0-8066-2497-3      LCCN 90-81702

Manufactured in the United Kingdom                    AF 9-2497

94   93   92   91   90   1   2   3   4   5   6   7   8   9   10